Hapsa Khan's little r

Ruwayda Mustafah
Lita Rizqiani

This book belongs to

....

To Baz, Anne and Adam,
My little tribe of joy

Hapsa Khan spent most of her afternoons in the garden, sitting in the cool shade of a tree, hearing birds chirp away, often with a welcome breeze. Her thirst for learning and knowledge were boundless, and she would often lose herself in the magic of stories.

After hours of reading, she would close her eyes, and imagine the stories in their vividness. Sometimes, she would be so deep in imagination that she'd fall asleep. Her heart would be fully content, because nothing made little Hapsa Khan happier than the magic of learning new things.

As soon as she finished a book, she would run along the fields and back home, to the delicious scent of Yaprax (Dolma) and cardamom tea filling the air.

When she arrived home, she would often find her father by the stove, waiting for her fascinating stories. "daddy, I want to share today's story with you," and out would pour her stories, as her father listened attentively, with the smell of a pot of Yaprax (Dolma) filling the room.

"Mama, the tea is delicious" Hapsa Khan loved having tea after a hearty meal, and she confided in her dearest mother, "I have many chapters left from my book to finish." "I'm so glad you are enjoying reading Hapsa gyan, but perhaps you should consider sharing your books with your friends, they would love it just as much," her mother replied.

Hapsa Khan spent the remainder of the evening reading while curled up in a soft blanket. She thought about her mother's advice, and decided that reading with her friends would surely be much more fun and exciting than reading just by herself.

As morning approached and Hapsa Khan enjoyed chai (tea), mast (yoghurt) and naan (bread) with her parents.

She put on her best Jili Kurdi (Kurdish traditional attire) and grabbed her favourite three books for her friends. Out she went, knocking door by door, asking them to join her in a session of reading together. Her friends, very much excited, joined her in the fields, and they all read to each other.

Note to parents

I hope you have enjoyed reading this short story as much as I have enjoyed writing it. I wrote it for my own children, Baz, Anne, and Adam because I wanted them to be familiar with the iconic Kurdistani characters that we are so proud of.

Our homeland, Kurdistan, is home to thousands of fascinating stories, and they're waiting to be written. This story is purely fictional, but the legend of it - known as Hapsa Khan - is very much real and a part of our collective history.

Hapsa Khan is a national Kurdistani icon. She founded the very first women's school in the entire of Iraq, and it was called the Kurdish Women's association.

She was born to a wealthy and prominent family in 1891 within the city of culture, Sulaimani. It is said that she was so passionate about young girls' literacy that she knocked door-to-door to persuade parents to send their children to her school.

I hope we can keep her memory alive by reading as much as possible - be it at home, with our families and friends or in our schools.

I would like to take this opportunity to support an upcoming and young artist in the Kurdistan Region, who has painted a beautiful canvas in tribute to the memory of Hapsa Khan. If you have a painting or drawing of Hapsa Khan, please send them to me (and perhaps it will be highlighted in future editions).

IG: @Lostincolors._

Nareen is a 21-year-old self-taught Kurdish painter who lives in Sulaimani, Kurdistan. She's a final-year engineering stu- dent and her works are mostly inspired by Kurdish culture and painted with acrylic. Her personal style spreads joy and peace and expresses the Kurdish spirit.